Lucy the Littlest Puppy

Lucy the Littlest Puppy

Holly Webb

Illustrated by Sophy Williams

SCHOLASTIC INC.

For William and Robin

ISBN 978-0-545-47437-5

Text copyright © 2011 by Holly Webb
Illustrations copyright © 2011 by Sophy Williams

12 11 10 9 8 7 6 5 4 3   13 14 15 16 17 18/0

Printed in the U.S.A.   40
First Scholastic printing, January 2013

Chapter One

"Bella's looking so fat!" Lauren peered under the kitchen table at Bella, the family's beagle. She was sitting in the middle of everyone's feet, panting and looking uncomfortable. Her tummy was huge, and the expression on her face was a little grumpy.

Dad checked under the table, too. "Well, she is due to have the puppies any day now. I'll take her temperature later on, to check if it's gone down."

Lauren nodded. They had been taking Bella's temperature every day for the last couple of weeks, since their vet, Mark, had told them it was the best way to tell if the puppies were about to come.

Bella padded heavily out from under the table and wandered over to her cushion. She took hold of the edge in her teeth—it was a big, soft cushion, made of red fabric—and tugged it closer to the radiator. Then she nudged it with her nose, this way and that, like she couldn't get it quite how she wanted it.

Lauren watched her hopefully. "Does that look like nesting to you?" she asked.

"I don't know. It might be . . ." her mom said doubtfully. It was the first time Bella had had puppies, and they were having to learn as they went along, even though Lauren's mom had bought three different books about dog breeding.

"We need to leave for school," Dad pointed out, checking his watch.

Lauren sighed. "I bet Bella will have the puppies while I'm at school, and I really, really want to be there. Couldn't I just stay home? It's the last day of school—we're not going to actually do anything, are we?"

Mom shook her head. "No. Besides, don't you want to say good-bye to all your friends? You might not see a lot of them for a while, remember."

Lauren frowned. It was true. She loved living way out in the country. Their home had been a farmhouse originally, and it had a huge yard. The old cowsheds had been made into her parents' office, and there was a barn across the yard that Lauren could play in. But there were bad things about it, too. She lived a twenty-minute drive from the town where her school was, and her best friend, Millie, lived about twenty minutes beyond the school in the other direction! So arranging to see Millie over break always meant a lot of planning.

Lauren got her bag and the present she'd gotten for her teacher, Ms. Ford, and took one last look at Bella on the way out the kitchen door. The beautiful brown-and-white dog was squirming around on her cushion as though she couldn't quite get comfy.

"Can you just hold on until I get home?" Lauren pleaded. But Bella looked up at her with big, mournful eyes. Lauren petted her lovingly. "I see what you mean. You must really want to be back to your old self again.

If it happens today, good luck, Bella. It'll be worth it—you're going to have beautiful puppies soon."

"She's going to be very tired," Dad pointed out. "We'll have to take care of her. I remember doing all this with Rusty, my parents' dog, when I was just a little older than you. Now come on, Lauren, we're going to be late."

As they were bumping down the lane toward the main road in their car, Lauren asked, "How many puppies do you think Bella will have?"

Dad shook his head. "Hard to tell— could be anything from one to fourteen, according to those books your mom bought. Rusty only had five."

Lauren frowned. "It can't just be one. Bella's enormous."

"I think you're probably right—she is very big. I'd say we're looking at quite a few," Dad agreed.

He sighed as he noted her sparkling eyes and excited smile. "Lauren . . ."

"What?" Lauren looked over at him worriedly.

"Sweetheart, just remember that we aren't keeping these puppies. They're all going to go to new homes."

Lauren hesitated for a moment. "I know," she said quietly. She was silent for a little while and then added, "But we'll have them for a couple of months, won't we? That's all of summer vacation to play with them."

Dad nodded. "Exactly. Of course we'll miss them when they go, but it'll be easier if we remember that they aren't ours to keep."

"I won't forget," Lauren promised. "Oh, there's Millie, Dad! Can you let me out here? I can walk up the road to school with her and her mom, can't I?"

Dad pulled up, and Lauren jumped out of the car, waving to her best friend.

"Hi! How's Bella? Have the puppies arrived yet?" Millie asked breathlessly.

Lauren shook her head, then smiled. "Bella was being really funny this morning. She kept messing around with her bed as if she was nesting. There might even be puppies when I get home!" she said, swinging her school bag excitedly.

"You're so lucky," said Millie. "Mom,

can we have one of Bella's puppies? Pleeeease?"

"Oh, Millie, you know I'd love one," said her mom, hitching Millie's baby sister, Amy, higher up on her hip. "But it just wouldn't be fair to have a dog —I'm busy with your sister, and your dad's at work during the day. A puppy would get lonely."

Millie sighed. "I guess you're right."

"You'll be able to play with them when you come over during break," Lauren promised her. "And I won't get to keep the puppies, either. Dad was reminding me in the car."

Millie nodded. "Still, you'll have weeks and weeks to play with them all. Oh, there's the bell. See you later, Mom!"

The two girls ran into class and joined the crowd of children around Ms. Ford, all begging her to open their good-bye present first.

Chapter Two

Lauren usually spent a long time chatting with all her friends after school, but today she was desperate to see if the puppies had arrived. She dashed out onto the playground to find Dad waiting by the gate. Millie chased after her.

"Has Bella had the puppies yet?" Lauren gasped. She'd been running so fast, she had to grab on to Dad's arm to stop herself from falling over.·

Dad steadied her, laughing. "Yes."

"How many?" Lauren squeaked excitedly.

Dad smiled. "Guess."

Lauren frowned. "Five?"

"Nowhere near. Ten!"

"Ten puppies?" Lauren turned toward Millie, her eyes round with amazement. "Ten? That's a *huge* litter!"

Millie laughed. "You'll have to think of ten names!"

"That's going to be tricky," Dad said. Lauren gave him a worried look. He didn't sound quite as happy as she thought the owner of ten puppies should. A sudden horrible thought hit her. Ten puppies was a lot—it must have been such hard work for Bella, giving birth to so many. What if something was wrong with her? Lauren opened her mouth to ask, and then shut it again. She didn't want to talk about something so scary in the middle of the school playground.

Instead, she hugged Millie good-bye and promised to e-mail her a picture of the puppies later.

But as soon as she and Dad were heading for the car, she grabbed his hand. "Dad, is everything okay?"

"What do you mean?" Dad looked at her carefully.

"I just thought you seemed a little worried—after you told us there were so many puppies. Is Bella all right?"

Dad gave her a hug. "Bella's fine. I mean, she's exhausted, but she did really well. It's not Bella. . . ." He hesitated. "Lauren, one of the puppies is a lot smaller than the others. Mom and I—we're not sure this one will make it. It's such a tiny scrap of a thing, and when it was first born, we weren't even sure if it was breathing. Bella had another puppy right after, and she didn't have time to lick the little puppy like she did with the others, or to bite through its cord. I had to cut the cord myself, and I rubbed the little pup with a washcloth to wake it up." He shook his head. "It did start to breathe, but it's not nearly as strong as the other puppies."

"Do you think it might die, Dad?" Lauren whispered.

Dad sighed. "I hope not—but we have to face the fact that it might."

"That's so sad." Lauren felt tears stinging her eyes. The poor little puppy.

"Nine healthy puppies is a great litter," Dad reminded her.

Lauren nodded. "I guess so. But I can't help worrying about the little one."

"I know—me too. Still, it might perk up. You never know."

Lauren crossed her fingers behind her back. She wanted Bella to have all ten of her wonderful puppies safe and well.

Lauren crept in the kitchen door. She was trying very hard not to bother Bella.

But Bella looked like she'd be impossible to disturb. She was stretched out flat on her side, fast asleep on the pile of old towels that Mom had put aside for her and the puppies to sleep on, in the special low wooden pen Dad had made for them. They'd been worried that the puppies might fall off Bella's big cushion.

The puppies were all snuggled up next to their mom, fast asleep in a pile of heads and paws. Lauren knelt down beside the pen and tried to count them, but she couldn't figure out where one puppy ended and the next began.

She couldn't see which was the little puppy that Dad was worried about, either.

"They're so tiny!" she whispered to Mom.

"I know, aren't they beautiful?" Mom beamed.

Lauren frowned. "They're all black and white! I can hardly see any brown on them at all. That's really weird, since Bella's brown and white."

Mom shook her head. "I thought that, too, but then I looked it up in our beagle book. It says they're usually born mostly black and white. The black might change to brown over the next few weeks, or stay as it is. Most beagles are black and white with brown patches —tricolor, it's called. Bella's coloring— just brown and white—is rare."

"Look how pink their noses are," Lauren breathed. "And I can hear them snuffling! They're so adorable."

"Aren't they?" Dad agreed. "Oh, look, Bella's waking up."

Lauren watched Bella yawn and blink sleepily, and crouched closer to the pen, expecting Bella to want to lick her hand. She was such a friendly dog, and she loved to cuddle up with Lauren

—preferably on the sofa watching cartoons.

But today Bella seemed to not see her. She was only interested in her puppies. She nudged them awake, pushing them gently toward her tummy so they could start feeding.

"She was like that with me, too," Mom murmured. "Not interested. It's as if she's only got eyes for her puppies now." She put her arm round Lauren's shoulders. "Don't worry. She'll only be like this for the first couple of weeks, until they open their eyes and start to move around. Then they won't need her so much, and she'll be our sweet Bella again."

Lauren nodded. "Can I pick up one of the puppies?" she asked. "Will Bella let us?"

"We haven't touched them yet," Dad said. "We didn't want to upset Bella."

Lauren peered at the pile of puppies as Bella woke them up. "Which is the little one—the one that was having trouble breathing?" she asked anxiously. "Oh! I think I can see—is it the one Bella's licking?"

Mom nodded. "Yes, that one's definitely a lot smaller than the others."

"Oh, look, you can see its little brown eyebrows!" Lauren said admiringly.

She edged closer to the pen, and Bella glanced up, as if to make sure she wasn't going to harm the puppies. Lauren shuffled back a little, and Bella quickly went back to licking and nudging at the tiny puppy. The others were all feeding already—Lauren could hear the strange, wheezy squeak as they sucked. She giggled. "Look, Mom, that puppy's sitting on the other one's head!"

Mom smiled. "I don't think they mind as long as they're getting their mom's milk."

Dad was looking at one of the others. "Hey, pup. I don't think that's going to do you much good." He chuckled. "Look, that big puppy's trying to suck Bella's paw."

Bella looked around at the sound of Dad's voice and spotted the confused puppy. She wrinkled her nose, and then gently pushed the puppy over to her tummy to feed with its brothers and sisters. Then she went back to trying to rouse the tiny pup.

"That one really is a lot smaller than

the others," Lauren said worriedly.

"And it's going to stay that way if it doesn't feed," Dad put in. "Oh, hang on—look. Bella's got it moving."

The littlest puppy scrabbled wearily, its paws waving. It was making sad squeaking sounds, like it wished Bella had let it just sleep, but at last it managed to burrow in among the rest of the litter.

"Is it feeding?" Mom asked hopefully.

"I think so." Lauren tried to listen for sucking sounds, but it was hard to tell with nine other puppies feeding at the same time. "Its head's moving backward and forward, like the others."

Dad nodded. "That's good—I was getting worried."

Then Lauren winced as one of the

other puppies kicked the tiny one in the stomach—not on purpose, since the bigger puppy was just scrambling to get back to Bella's milk. The tiny puppy lay there, kicking feebly, and then it seemed to go back to sleep. Lauren watched anxiously, willing it to wake up and feed again. But the littlest puppy just lay where it was, while its brothers and sisters wriggled and kicked for the best spot.

Chapter Three

Hi Millie,

Here's a photo of the newborn puppies! I bet you can't count all ten in this picture, though. They're all cuddled up together. They're really adorable, but there's one tiny one that's having touble feeding. I just hope it's going to get better. Please come and see the puppies soon.

Love, Lauren

Lauren sent her e-mail to Millie and went downstairs to find Dad making dinner and Mom cuddling one of the puppies. Bella sat at the edge of the pen and kept a close eye on her.

"Oh, wow, she let you pick one up!"

Mom nodded. "But I was very careful. I washed my hands, and then I petted Bella first, so that I didn't make the puppy smell like me. The book I was reading said that it was good to start handling puppies early, to get them used to people, but I don't want to worry Bella. She doesn't seem too bothered, though—we thought she would be okay, since she's such a friendly dog." Mom ran her finger very gently down the snoozing puppy's back. "If you wash your hands, you can pet the puppy, too."

Lauren carefully washed her hands, and made a fuss of Bella first, petting her with both hands to get Bella's scent on her fingers. Then she petted the puppy with one finger, like her mom had. It felt like slightly damp velvet—and it was no bigger than one of the Beanie toy dogs she had on her windowsill upstairs. "It's so soft. . . ." she breathed.

Bella made a little snorting noise and lay down next to her puppies again, but she was still eyeing Lauren and her mom.

"Look how fat its tummy is," Mom pointed out. "This puppy's absolutely stuffed."

"I think we should put it back," Lauren said. "Bella looks a little worried. But she hasn't growled or anything. She's such a good dog."

"And a good mother, too," Dad said from over by the stove. "She's taken to it so well."

Lauren's mom gently slipped the puppy back into the pen next to Bella, who licked it all over. The puppy made a squeaking noise as Bella's big tongue licked its head, but it didn't wake up.

"Where's the tiny one?" Lauren asked, trying to count the puppies.

Mom frowned. "I'm sure I saw it just a moment ago. I think it had some more milk, which is really good. Apparently Bella's milk is full of all sorts of good stuff on the day they're born. The puppies get all the benefits of the vaccinations she's had, and that kind of thing."

"I can't see the little puppy now," Lauren muttered anxiously. "What if it's under all the others and they squish it?"

Mom knelt down next to her. "Isn't that it?" she asked, pointing to a puppy.

Lauren shook her head. "No, it has brown eyebrows, remember? That one's just black and white."

"Oh, yes." Mom edged around to

the other side of the pen. "It's here, look, behind Bella. It must have gotten pushed out of the way by the others."

Lauren followed her, moving slowly so she wouldn't disturb Bella. "Is it okay?"

Bella was watching carefully, and as soon as she realized what had happened, she wriggled around and tried to nudge the puppy over with her nose. But the puppy was fast asleep and didn't move. Bella glanced up at Lauren and her mom, almost as though she wasn't quite sure what to do.

"Should we move the puppy for her?" Lauren asked, frowning.

Mom was starting to say, "Maybe we should . . ." when Bella leaned down and picked up the tiny puppy in her mouth.

"Mom, what's Bella doing?" Lauren whispered in horror.

"Don't worry," Mom soothed her. "It's fine. Dogs do that, Lauren—she won't hurt the puppy."

But it didn't look at all comfortable. The puppy's legs dangled out on either side of Bella's mouth, and it wheezed and squeaked unhappily. Bella swiftly tucked it in along the row of teats on her tummy, and watched hopefully.

Lauren and Mom watched, too, and Dad left the pasta sauce he was stirring and came to peer over their shoulders, holding a tomatoey wooden spoon.

"It's feeding," Lauren whispered excitedly, seeing the little shoulders moving.

Mom nodded. "And since all the others are asleep, hopefully it'll be able to keep feeding for a while."

"Oh, that's good." Dad sighed with relief. "And good timing. Dinner's ready."

Lauren went to bed that night very reluctantly. She wanted to stay and watch the puppies, especially the tiniest one. She was still worried that it wasn't getting enough milk. Because it wasn't as big as the others, it couldn't wriggle its way back to Bella's teats when it got pushed away, like the others could. Instead of barging past its brothers and sisters, the littlest puppy would just whine miserably and go back to sleep.

"Can't I stay up a bit longer? It's the first day of vacation tomorrow," Lauren begged.

"It's already an hour later than bedtime!" Mom pointed out. "You can come down early in the morning to see them. But now you need to go to bed."

Lauren sighed, recognizing Mom's no-argument voice. Still, she was sure she wouldn't ever fall asleep.

Lauren woke up suddenly and found her bedroom in darkness. So she *had* fallen asleep after all.

She sat up, hugging her knees. What time was it? It felt like the middle of the night. She glanced at her luminous clock. Two o'clock in the morning. Lauren shuddered. No wonder it was so dark. She lay down again, but she didn't feel sleepy anymore. Something was worrying her, and she wasn't sure what it was. Then she realized—the puppies! Of course, how could she have forgotten about them?

She couldn't hear any noise from downstairs. Bella and the puppies were probably fast asleep. But she couldn't stop feeling like something was wrong, and that was why she had woken up.

It wouldn't hurt to go and have a look, would it? Lauren smiled to herself —Mom had said she could come down early to see the puppies, after all. She probably hadn't meant quite this early, but still . . .

She got out of bed and crept over to her door, quickly pulling on her robe. As she ran across the landing to the stairs, she could hear her dad snoring. She hurried down the stairs and into the kitchen. She could make out little squeaks and sucking noises— the puppies were awake and feeding, but that wasn't really surprising. Lauren had been reading Mom's puppy books, and it said that for the first couple of weeks they would need to feed every two hours.

Mom had left a small lamp from the living room plugged in on the counter, so Bella had a little light for feeding the puppies. Bella was lying on her side looking sleepy, but she thumped her tail gently on the floor of the pen when she saw Lauren.

"Hey, Bella. I just came to see how you all are," Lauren whispered, kneeling beside the pen.

Bella closed her eyes wearily as Lauren patted her head and leaned over to count the puppies. Then she counted them again. Only nine!

Where was the little puppy with the brown eyebrows?

"Oh, Bella, where did it go?" Lauren whispered, but Bella was half-asleep, and she only twitched her tail.

Lauren checked behind Bella, where the puppy had ended up before, but there was nothing there. She was sure the other puppies weren't lying on the little one, and it couldn't possibly have climbed out. Frantically, Lauren started to feel around the shadowy edges of the box.

"Oh!" Lauren gasped as she touched something little and soft, pushed away in the corner. "There you are!" She picked up the puppy, waiting for it to squeak and complain, but it didn't make a sound. "Oh, no, I didn't wash my hands—I suppose it's too late now." Lauren lifted the puppy up to see better, and realized that it was saggy and cold in her hands.

"Oh, no, please . . ." she murmured, and snuggled the puppy in a fold of her robe. "Mom! Dad!" she yelled as she raced back up the stairs. "We need to call the vet!"

Chapter Four

"It woke up a little bit while I was holding it," Lauren explained to Mark, the vet. "Is it going to be all right?"

Mark put away his stethoscope and looked at the puppy thoughtfully. "You did a good thing catching her when you did, Lauren. She's a she, by the way."

Lauren smiled, just a little. She had thought the puppy was a she—it was something about those cute brown eyebrows.

"It looks to me like she was slipping away," Mark went on, gently petting the puppy's head. "Puppies can't control how warm or cold they are—they need their mom to keep them warm. You cuddling her warmed her up again. The real problem is that she's not strong enough to feed well by herself. But you could hand-raise her." He glanced up at Lauren, and her mom and dad. "I can't promise she'll make it. But it's worth a try. It's a lot of work, though."

Lauren's dad frowned. "What does hand-raising mean, exactly? I've taken care of puppies before, but I've never had to hand-raise one. Would we feed her with a bottle?"

"A baby bottle?" Lauren asked, looking at the tiny puppy. She was about the same size as a baby bottle!

Mark shook his head. "No, a special puppy one. I've got one somewhere." He rooted around in his bag. "Here it is. I stopped into the office when you called, and picked up some puppy milk replacement and some advice on hand-raising." He handed Lauren's dad a jar of white powder and a leaflet. "You mix it with water, just like baby formula. Puppies can't drink cow's milk—it's got the wrong mix of nutrients."

Lauren's dad read the instructions on the jar. "Every two hours?" he asked, sounding slightly worried.

"Only for the first week," Mark reassured him. "After that you'll probably be able to leave her without feeding her through the middle of the night."

Dad rubbed his eyes wearily—it was now four o'clock in the morning. He and Mom ran their own mail-order business from home, and he'd been up late checking orders. He nodded. "Well, that's what we'll do." He glanced at Mom, who was looking anxious. "We can't not," he added gently.

Mom nodded. "Of course. It's going to be hard, though." She smiled at Lauren. "A little bit like when you were a baby."

Mark smiled. "But puppies grow faster than babies. They stop drinking their mom's milk at about seven weeks old. This little one should be feeding herself before you know it."

Lauren nodded. She hoped it worked. Mark hadn't sounded absolutely sure that it would. But Lauren had already saved this puppy once, and if she had anything to do with it, the little one was going to make it.

"I'll do it," she said to her parents. "The feeding, I mean. I don't mind."

"You can't get up every two hours in the middle of the night!" Mom said, sounding horrified.

Lauren went over to fill the kettle. "We should feed her now, shouldn't we? Do we have to use boiled water? Like Millie's mom uses for her little sister's bottles?"

Mark grinned at Lauren's parents. "It sounds like Lauren knows what she's doing."

Lauren beamed at him. She really wanted to help, but she had a feeling Mom and Dad were going to be reluctant about it. "Do we have to keep the puppy separate from the others?" she asked, trying hard to think of anything else they might need to know.

Mark frowned. "I would for tonight. She's obviously having trouble keeping warm, so she'll need a box and a hot-water bottle. Look, the leaflet shows you. But after tonight, she'd be better off staying with her mom and the rest of the puppies, if she can. Just take her out for feeding. Best of luck, and if there are any problems, give the office a call."

The boiled water took a long time to cool down, and Lauren kept wanting to blow on it.

Mom went to prepare a box for the puppy, and Dad sat at the kitchen table reading the instruction leaflet Mark had left. "Small cardboard box. Blanket. Hot-water bottle," he muttered. "We should have thought about all of this before, but it just never crossed my mind that we'd have so many and Bella wouldn't be able to feed them all. Uuugh!"

"What?" Lauren turned around, still cradling the puppy.

Dad was making a face. "According to this leaflet, we're going to have to help the puppy do its business. . . . They don't do it themselves, apparently, so because Bella won't be licking her after she's fed, we'll have to wipe around her bottom with wet cotton balls."

Lauren made a face back. That *was* a little yucky. But it didn't put her off. She was going to do anything she had to to keep the puppy going. Even if that meant making her go to the bathroom.

"I think this water's cool enough to mix the formula now. Not long till you can have some milk, Lucy."

"Lucy?" Mom asked. "When did you name her?"

Lauren looked up. "I didn't even notice I had! But don't you think she looks like her name's Lucy?"

Mom nodded, but she was frowning, and Lauren bit her lip. She had a horrible feeling that Mom hadn't wanted her to name the tiny puppy in case she didn't make it.

Lauren carefully spooned the powder into the bottle and mixed in the water. "Wake up, little one. . . . Does it say how to hold her, Dad?"

Her dad skimmed through the instructions. "Flat, on her tummy, not on her back like a human baby. Here, look, on a towel." He laid a towel over Lauren's knees, and Lauren set Lucy down on her tummy. Her paws splayed out and she scrabbled a little and let out a tiny squeak, unsure what was going on.

"It's okay." Lauren picked up the bottle and gently put it against Lucy's mouth.

"Squeeze the bottle a little," Mom suggested. "She doesn't know what it is. Let her taste a few drops of the milk."

All of a sudden Lucy started to suck eagerly as she tasted the milk in her mouth. Her tiny pink paws, with their little transparent claws, pattered against Lauren's fingers, making her giggle. "Wow, she was ready for that."

Lucy took only five minutes to down the bottle.

"Goodness, should we give her some

more?" Mom asked.

Lauren shook her head. "No, this is how much Mark said for now. The tub of powder says how much you give for what size of puppy over a whole day, and then you have to divide that up between the feedings." She gave a big yawn, and on her knee, Lucy did the same.

Mom laughed. "I think we should all

go to bed. Especially if we have to be up at six-thirty to feed her again."

Lauren looked up at her mom hopefully. "Mom, my bedroom's nice and warm, and if I have her box in there, I can keep an eye on her. . . ."

"But we have to feed her so early. You don't want to get up at six-thirty on vacation!" Dad smiled.

"I do, I really do!" Lauren promised. "I was the one who woke up and found her, Dad. I really want to help."

Dad looked over at Lauren's mom. "What do you think, Annie?"

Mom sighed. "I suppose so. But only for tonight, Lauren. Tomorrow, when she's a little stronger, Lucy can go back with Bella and the other puppies."

Lauren nodded eagerly and picked

up the cardboard box. Inside, Lucy was snuggling up against the well-wrapped hot-water bottle. She looked happier than she had all day, Lauren thought. She padded back up the stairs, yawning uncontrollably. She set the box down next to her bed and fell asleep listening to the tiny wheezing breaths from inside the box.

It was really hard to get up when Dad came in at six-thirty A.M., but Lauren dragged herself out of bed and carried Lucy's box downstairs to watch Dad make up her next bottle. The trip downstairs hadn't disturbed Lucy at all, she noticed with a smile. The puppy was still snoozing peacefully next to the cooling hot-water bottle.

In the kitchen, Bella was out of the puppy pen looking hungry, and Lauren fed her while Dad boiled the water.

"Can I feed Lucy again?" Lauren begged, and Dad handed her the bottle.

"You might as well—you certainly seemed to have the knack earlier!"

Going downstairs might not have woken Lucy, but the smell of the puppy formula certainly did, and she was gasping and squeaking with excitement as soon as Lauren held the bottle to her mouth.

After she'd cleaned Lucy up, Lauren took her over to Bella. She and Dad hovered anxiously, not too close to the puppy pen, watching to see how Bella would react.

"I hope Lucy will be all right," Lauren muttered. "It said in that leaflet that sometimes the mom tries to lick the human smell away and accidentally hurts the puppy."

Dad put an arm around her shoulders. "We'll watch really carefully," he promised. "And it's not as if Bella's a dog at a big breeder's who lives outside and doesn't really know people that well. She's part of our family. Hopefully our smell won't upset her too much."

"Look!" Lauren whispered.

Bella was sniffing thoughtfully at Lucy, and Lauren held her breath as Bella started to lick the little puppy. But Bella didn't look at all upset, just a little surprised.

Lauren giggled. "Bella's so worn out, I bet she hardly noticed Lucy was gone!"

Over the next few days, Lauren was sure that Lucy had started to recognize her. If Lucy started squeaking in her box, she would calm down as soon as Lauren picked her up, but not if it was Mom or Dad. Lauren knew it was probably just that Lucy recognized her by smell as the person who usually fed her, but it still made her feel special. She couldn't wait for Lucy to open her eyes so that the puppy could see her as well as smell her.

Mom and Dad were supposed to be taking turns doing the night feedings, but Lauren couldn't help waking up when she heard the alarm go off in their bedroom. And once she was awake, she just couldn't stay in bed. Mom even stopped scolding her about it by the end of their second night of hand-raising the puppy.

Lucy was putting on weight now, although not as fast as the other puppies, who were fat and glossy-furred. She loved eating, but Lauren suspected she might always be a bit smaller than her brothers and sisters.

Lucy squeaked and sucked at Lauren's fingers as Lauren scooped her up. She knew Lauren's scent, and she was sure it was time for Lauren to feed her, and she was so, so hungry.

Lauren giggled as Lucy's little pink paws flailed around. "I'm just waiting for it to cool down. You don't want to burn your mouth!"

Lucy squeaked even louder. Where was the milk?

"Okay, okay, here you go."

Lucy sighed happily, and settled down to sucking. That was much better.

After the first week, Lauren and her parents could leave Lucy for six hours in the middle of the night without a bottle. Dad said he'd do the midnight feeding on his own—he was used to staying up late working, anyway. Lauren had to admit it was really nice to get a full night's sleep again, even though she still had to get up super-early for Lucy's morning bottle.

Millie came to visit the puppies when they were about two weeks old.

"Can I feed Lucy?" she asked hopefully. "That photo you sent me of you feeding her was so cute. She's even more adorable now that her eyes are open, though."

"She is, isn't she?" Lauren agreed, handing Millie the bottle.

Lucy watched Lauren the whole time she was feeding, and Lauren could tell she was a little confused why somebody else was holding her bottle.

"You have to burp her now, like your mom burps Amy!" Lauren told Millie, when Lucy had finished.

Now that the puppies were two weeks old, their eyes were open, although they still hadn't started to move around much. The really exciting thing was that their markings were starting to come through. Lucy had more brown on her face now, not just her pretty eyebrows, and all the puppies were changing every day.

Even though the puppies were still too tiny to really play with, Millie didn't want to leave when her mom came to pick her up.

Lauren waved good-bye from

the door, and sighed as Millie's car disappeared down the road. She really missed seeing her best friend every day.

"Lauren, I've got some really exciting news," her mom started as she came back into the kitchen. "Hey, what's the matter?"

"I just wish I could see Millie more often over vacation, that's all. E-mail and the phone aren't the same as having a friend close by."

Her mom gave her a hug. "This is going to be extra-good news for you, then." She beamed at Lauren. "We've rented out the cottage. To a family with a boy the same age as you!"

Lauren blinked. The cottage was on the other side of the orchard, just beyond the farmyard. The old tenant had left a while ago, and Lauren had forgotten they were trying to find someone new.

"He's named Sam Martin, and he's got a little sister named Molly. Isn't that wonderful? You'll have a friend really close by!"

Lauren nodded slowly, but she wasn't sure it was all that wonderful. What if she didn't like this boy? And even if she did, he wouldn't be as good a friend as Millie.

Chapter Five

"Oh, that sounds like the Martins at the door!" Mom fussed around the kitchen and said, "Would you open it, Lauren?"

It was two weeks after Mom had broken the news about the new neighbors moving in, and they'd said they were going to stop by that afternoon. Lauren still couldn't help wishing it was a girl her age rather than a boy. And she didn't want some strange boy and his little sister messing around with Lucy and upsetting her. Instead of opening the door, she quickly dashed upstairs with Lucy and stashed her in the box she'd slept in on the first night. Mom still let her take Lucy upstairs occasionally, and Lucy couldn't get out of the box yet, although she really liked trying.

Lucy whined in surprise as Lauren put her down. What was happening? She had been having a nice cuddle, and now she was being left all on her own! She stood up with her paws against the edge of the box, scrabbling hard. Where was Lauren? She whimpered miserably.

Lauren ran back downstairs and tried to look friendly as Mom introduced her to Nicky Martin and Sam, a blond-haired boy who looked just as embarrassed as she felt. Sam's dad was still figuring things out at the house, and his little sister was asleep, Nicky said.

Sam cuddled one of the puppies, the big boy that they had named Buster, and didn't really say much. Lauren was just hoping that they might go soon— surely they must have a lot of unpacking to do? But then her mom nudged her and said meaningfully, "Why don't you show Sam around the farm?"

Lauren frowned. It was almost time to feed Lucy, and she didn't want to show him around anyway!

Her mom glared at her, and she gave a tiny sigh and turned to Sam. "Come on. You can bring Buster, if you like."

Sam nodded and followed her out into the yard. "He's really nice. Is he your favorite?"

Lauren shook her head.

"Don't you have a favorite? He'd be mine—he's great." Sam snuggled Buster up under his chin.

Lauren didn't know what to say.

It would sound stupid to admit she'd hidden Lucy away. "I like them all," she said vaguely.

Lauren trailed around the farm, showing Sam the orchard, and the old barn on the other side of the yard. There were a few bales of hay in it still, and she liked to hide out in there sometimes.

"This is cool. I bet the puppies would love it in here," said Sam.

Lauren nodded. "They haven't been outside much yet, but Dad's fencing off an area for them to play in the orchard."

Sam looked up. "Oh, that's my mom calling. I guess we have to go and unpack."

He handed Buster to Lauren, and they headed back to the farmhouse. Lauren thought Sam was okay— at least he liked the puppies—but she didn't think they were going to be best friends or anything, which was obviously what Mom was hoping.

"He was nice, wasn't he?" Mom asked as they waved good-bye to Sam and his mom. "Gosh, look at Buster!" She tickled the puppy under the chin. "He's huge. I've got to look into putting an ad in the local paper about new homes for the puppies. And there are a couple of good puppy websites, too."

Lauren swallowed. Her heart seemed to have suddenly jumped into her throat. New homes! She had almost forgotten about that—she had wanted to forget.

"But they're only a month old, Mom!" she cried.

"I know. But puppies go to their new owners at about eight weeks, and people don't just turn up and take a puppy home. We'll have to let them come and see the puppies—and we need to meet the people to make sure we like them." She hugged Lauren. "We're not going to give Bella's lovely puppies to just anyone, sweetheart, don't worry."

Lauren nodded. "But—but not Lucy, right?" she asked quickly. "She isn't big enough yet, Mom."

Mom nodded thoughtfully. "You're probably right. Lucy will have to be a little older than the others when she goes. Not much, though, I shouldn't think. You've done so well feeding her, she's catching up to them." She looked at Lauren. "I know you really love Lucy, and it'll be hard for you to say good-bye, but you'll still have Bella, remember."

Lauren buried her nose in Buster's soft fur. She loved Bella, of course she did. But Lucy would have died if Lauren hadn't woken up that first night. It felt like she and Lucy belonged together. But Lauren just didn't think she could explain that to Mom.

She put Buster back in the puppy pen, and ran upstairs to get Lucy. When she opened her bedroom door, Lucy scrabbled at the side of the box with her claws, squeaking frantically.

"Oh, I'm sorry. I went off and left you, didn't I?" Lauren scooped up the puppy, her eyes filling with tears. "I didn't mean to." She sighed, feeling Lucy wriggle and squirm against her neck. "I don't ever want to leave you. But I'm not going to, am I? You're going to leave me. Oh, Lucy, I don't want you to go!"

Summer vacation seemed to have gone by so quickly, Lauren thought. She could hardly believe there was less than a week to go until school started! She guessed it felt fast because she'd been busy the whole time taking care of Lucy and Bella, and the other puppies.

Lucy's brothers and sisters loved the little outdoor run that Lauren's dad had made for them, and spent lots of time out there now. Lauren's mom had put a photo of them all romping around on the grass on the pet website where she was advertising them to new owners.

Lauren wasn't sure about letting Lucy go out in the run yet—she was still so much smaller than the other puppies, and Lauren was worried that they might hurt her with their rough and tumble games.

"Mom, can I take Lucy out to play in the orchard, if I'm really careful not to let her run off?"

Her mom put down the phone. "Yes, that's fine. Although I'm sure she'd be all right in the run with the others, you know. She's a lot bigger now."

Lauren sighed. Lucy *was* catching up. But she still wouldn't feed from Bella like they did. Dad said she liked her special bottles too much. They wouldn't have to do the bottle feedings for too much longer, though. Now that the puppies were five weeks old, they were all eating solid food, too. Lauren loved to watch them all eat. The first few meals had gone everywhere but into the puppies' mouths, and Bella had ended up having most of it as she'd licked it off the puppies. They had the same dry food as Bella, but mixed with the puppy milk Lucy had, and they always ended up with mush caked all over their ears.

"Who was on the phone?" Lauren asked as she finished her toast. "It wasn't someone calling about the puppies, was it?"

"No, it was just Nicky, Sam's mom. We'd talked about sharing the drive to school next week, and she wanted to know if we'd rather do morning or afternoon. I said we'd pick you up in the afternoon, is that okay? I like hearing about your day."

Lauren gaped at her. "Sam's going to my school?" she asked.

"Well, of course he is. Yours is the only school close by."

"He's not in my class, is he?"

"No, he's in the other class in your grade." Her mom frowned. "His mom and I talked about it when they came over—didn't you hear us?"

Lauren shook her head. She'd probably been too busy being grumpy about having to entertain Sam. And now she had to share rides to school with him! She knew it would make less work for Mom and Dad, but she didn't want to share her car trips; she liked having the time to chat with them.

Grumpy, she picked up Lucy and

a ball from the puppy pen and stomped out into the yard.

Lucy squirmed excitedly in Lauren's arms, sniffing all the interesting new smells. She'd been everywhere in the house with Lauren, but this was different. A butterfly fluttered past, and she yapped at it in delight. When they got to the orchard, which had a brick wall all around it, Lauren gently put her down on the grass.

Lucy looked up at her, not sure what she was supposed to do. She gave an inquiring little whine.

"Go play!" Lauren rolled the ball, and Lucy chased after it, yapping. She tried to sink her teeth into it, but it was just too big, and she ended up rolling over on top of the ball with a squeak of dismay.

Lucy bounced up and went off sniffing around in the grass, until she came to a dock plant, with big shield-shaped leaves. She licked a leaf thoughtfully, and then seized it in her teeth, pulling hard. It sprang back, and she jumped around yapping fiercely, until Lauren nearly choked with laughter.

All of a sudden there was a heavy thud, and a big soccer ball bounced over the orchard wall and thumped onto the grass right next to Lucy, who whimpered in fright. She scampered over to Lauren.

Lauren snatched Lucy up in one arm, grabbed the ball with the other, and ran across to the wall to find Sam peering over it.

"Hey! You almost hit Lucy with that! What are you doing?" Lauren snapped.

"Sorry! I was just kicking the ball around. . . ." Sam looked guilty.

"You could have hurt her!" Lauren told him as she shoved the ball into his hands.

"Sorry . . ." Sam muttered again, and he walked away with his shoulders hunched up.

Lauren almost felt sorry for yelling at him, but then Lucy wriggled into her neck, whimpering, and Lauren felt angry all over again.

When school started the next week, Lauren had to carpool with Sam, as her mom had arranged, but Lauren hardly talked to him. She didn't really know what to say, and Sam seemed shy. Getting angry with him in the orchard probably didn't help.

It was great being back at school and seeing all her friends again, but she really missed Lucy and the other puppies.

"Are they big enough for new homes yet?" Millie asked during recess.

"Mom's got people coming to see them already, and they can leave Bella after next week, she says. People have already chosen six of them. Not Lucy, though—she's still too little." *Thank goodness*, she added silently. Over the weekend, a family had come to see the puppies, and the little girl had picked up Lucy, saying she wanted her. Lauren had felt sick. Luckily, Mom had seen her horrified face and explained that Lucy was too small to go for a few more weeks. The family had chosen two girl puppies named Daisy and Danni instead. But afterward Mom had sat down with Lauren and hugged her, and explained that she was going to have to let Lucy go sometime.

"You'll really miss her, won't you?" Millie said, putting her arm through Lauren's, and Lauren nodded.

"Couldn't you ask your mom and dad if you can keep her?" Millie suggested.

"I wish I could," Lauren whispered. "They've always said we can't, that we already have Bella. But I just can't bear to think of Lucy belonging to someone else."

Chapter Six

Lucy watched the strange boy cuddling Buster and wondered who he was. There were lots of other people in her kitchen, too, but they all seemed friendly. Everyone who had come to the house over the last two weeks had wanted to pet her and her brothers and sisters, and play with them. It was fun, but it was confusing, too. She had a feeling that this boy was going to take Buster away. He had been here before, and this time he had picked Buster up right away, and Buster had wagged his tail and yipped happily, the way Lucy did when Lauren cuddled her.

If Buster went away with this boy, then she would be the only puppy left. Daisy and Danni had gone with a little girl the day before. The girl's mother had put them in a special box with a wire front, and Lauren had taken Lucy out to see Daisy and Danni drive off in a car. Lauren had hugged her extra tight, and seemed really sad, although she'd cheered up and giggled when Lucy licked her ear.

Lucy missed rolling over and over with all the others, now that it was just her and Buster. She still had Lauren to play with, of course, and that was her favorite thing. But was she going to go somewhere, too, like all her brothers and sisters? She didn't want to. She wanted to stay here with Lauren.

The boy snuggled Buster under his chin, and then turned to put him into a carrier like the one Daisy and Danni went away in. Lucy watched them go out into the yard. Then she looked around the puppy pen, with its rumpled blankets and scattered toys, and howled a big beagle howl.

"Oh! Did Buster go today?" Lauren asked in surprise when she got home—she had been at Millie's house after school.

"Yes—only Lucy is left," her mom answered. "Did you have a good time?"

"Yes, it was great," Lauren replied, only half listening. She was looking at Lucy curled up asleep on the fluffy bed at one side of the puppy pen. She seemed so tiny and alone.

Lucy woke up and stared around at the empty pen, looking confused. She let out a tiny whimper and staggered to her feet, sniffing around the pen. Bella leaned over and licked her gently, and Lucy stopped whimpering, but she still looked uncertain.

Mom put her arm around Lauren. "She's gotten so much bigger, hasn't she? And you can really see all the brown coming out on her now. She's going to be so beautiful. You did really well hand-raising her, Lauren, and it was such hard work. Dad and I are very proud of you, you know."

"Thanks," Lauren muttered. She was proud of what she'd managed with Lucy, too, but she had a horrible feeling that she knew what was coming next.

"I know you'll miss her, sweetheart, but she's ready to go to a new home, isn't she?" Mom said gently. "She's hardly interested in her bottles, and she's eating dry food now."

Lauren nodded, and sniffed. It was all true, but that didn't make it any easier. She pulled away from her mom with a muttered, "Sorry!" picked up Lucy, who squeaked in surprise, and fled upstairs.

Lauren was really looking forward to Friday and the start of the weekend. She enjoyed being back at school, but she missed Lucy so much—and she wasn't sure how much more time they had together.

Her dad had picked up her and Sam as usual, and they sat in the back-seat while Dad tried to ask cheerful questions about how Sam was settling in. Sam kept responding with things like, "Okay," and, "Fine, thanks."

They dropped Sam off, and then Lauren ran inside to say hello to Lucy.

The phone was ringing as she went into the kitchen, and her mom yelled from upstairs, "Can you answer that, Lauren? I'm making the beds!"

Lauren grabbed the phone, hoping it wasn't an order for her parents' camping supplies company, since she always worried she'd get them wrong.

"Hello?"

"Is this Mrs. Woods? With the beagle puppies?"

"Oh! Yes—I mean, I'm her daughter," Lauren explained.

"Oh, good. Do you have any puppies left? I just saw the ad."

Lauren swallowed. This lady might end up being Lucy's owner. All of a sudden her eyes filled with tears. "There is one puppy left," she said, making her voice sound very doubtful.

"Okay—is there something wrong with it?" The lady on the phone sounded worried.

"We-ell . . . She was the smallest of the litter—much smaller than the others. We had to hand-raise her."

"Oh, dear. Well, if she's not healthy I think I'll try someone else. Thanks, anyway."

Lauren pressed the button to end the call with a shaky hand, and put down the phone.

But she couldn't answer the phone every time someone called. . . .

Still feeling really guilty, Lauren took Lucy out into the yard to play. She threw a ball for Lucy to chase, and Lucy raced up and down the lawn with excited squeaks.

"Lauren!" Mom was calling from the side yard of the house, where the clothesline was. "Can you help me hang up the wash, please?"

Lauren sighed. Hanging up the wash was one of the jobs she did to earn her allowance. "Sorry, Lucy," she said, picking her up. "You go in the run, okay? I'll be back soon."

Lucy stared after her, whining. Lauren had left the ball on the grass, and there were no toys in the run. Lucy ran up and down, sniffing at the wire, then scratched at it, wondering if she

could get out and fetch the ball. She
stuck a small paw through the wire fence,
but the ball was too far away to reach.

Lucy yapped, frustrated. She
scratched at the wire again, standing
up on her hind paws. Her claws
caught in the wire. She looked at them
thoughtfully, and unhooked them.
Then she stretched up higher, clinging
on tight. She was climbing! Wriggling
and scrambling, she worked her way up
the side of the run. She teetered on the
top, not quite sure what
to do next. All at
once, she let go
and scrambled
down the other
side, landing in
a little heap.

She sprang up and shook herself excitedly. There it was—her ball! She chased after it, scrabbling it along with her front paws, and followed the ball as it rolled ahead.

Ten minutes later, Lauren dashed back, eager to continue playing with Lucy, only to find that Lucy wasn't there.

She stood staring at the run. The fence was about a foot high—Lucy couldn't climb over that, right?

"Lucy! Lucy!" Lauren cried as she ran all around the run.

But the little puppy was nowhere to be seen.

Chapter Seven

Lucy pattered across the yard and set off to explore around the other side of the orchard wall. She'd abandoned the ball in favor of all the other interesting things she could smell. Maybe she'd find Lauren if she went down here, too. She spotted a snail climbing up the wall and watched it, round-eyed. She went closer and sniffed. It had an odd smell, and she decided it wasn't for eating.

"Hey! Lucy!" Lucy jumped, and looked up. That wasn't Lauren's voice.

It was the boy, Sam, holding a big ball. She'd seen him before when he came to the house to fetch Lauren in the mornings. She sniffed his fingers in a friendly sort of way. Maybe he would play with her?

"Are you supposed to be out here on your own?" he asked. "I bet you're not."

"Lucy! Lucy!" There was a distant voice calling, sounding worried.

"You're definitely not," Sam told Lucy. "That sounds like Lauren looking for you."

Lucy could hear Lauren, too, but she wasn't quite sure where she was. She whimpered anxiously.

"It's all right. Let's find Lauren, okay?" Sam looked down at her, and Lucy pawed his foot eagerly.

"Come on, then. Good girl." Sam put down the ball and picked up Lucy. He walked quickly down to the yard. "Hey, Lauren, I've got her!"

Lauren came dashing out of her yard. She grabbed Lucy, hugging her tightly while the puppy whined with delight. "Oh, you're the best, Sam! I was really worried. She must have climbed out of her run. Thanks!"

"Beagles are really good at escaping." Sam nodded, and Lauren looked at him in surprise. "I really like dogs," he explained. "We can't have one, because Dad's allergic, but I've got a ton of dog books. And I once saw a video on a website of a beagle climbing out of a massive pen."

"Oh." Lauren suddenly felt really ashamed. She'd been going to school with Sam every day, and she hadn't asked him anything about himself, or said a single friendly thing. "It's so great that you found her. What if she had gone onto the road?"

Sam nodded. "I can't imagine losing a dog like that," he agreed. "It would be awful."

Lauren's eyes suddenly welled up.

"Sorry! I didn't mean to make you cry!" Sam said, looking horrified.

"It's okay," Lauren gulped. "It's just— you don't understand. . . ." She wiped her hand across her eyes, while Lucy licked at her cheek anxiously.

"Lucy isn't mine. Not forever. She's going to have a new home, just like the other puppies. And I can't bear the thought of not having her anymore."

"Oh, wow," Sam muttered. "I thought you were keeping her, when she stayed and all the others went. And she's with you all the time."

"I've always known she'd have to go, like her brothers and sisters," Lauren whispered. "I still have Bella, and of course I love her, but I've spent so much time with Lucy, because we hand-raised her. It's going to be awful when she leaves. It was bad enough when people came for the others, but Lucy's special." She opened the orchard gate and gently shooed Lucy in. "Want to come and play with her?" she said.

Sam nodded and followed her. "Has anyone come to see Lucy?" he asked.

Lauren shook her head. "Someone called earlier, and I sort of mentioned how Lucy was the runt of the litter and made this lady think she wasn't very healthy. . . ."

She glanced at Sam, not sure what he'd think, but Sam looked impressed.

"I felt really guilty afterward," Lauren admitted. "And I can't keep putting people off."

Sam looked thoughtful. "There must be something you can do. I'll help you." He looked at Lucy, who was destroying an apple on the ground. "You can't lose her," he said firmly.

Lauren smiled. He sounded so certain it made her feel a little bit better.

The next morning, Sam knocked at the kitchen door while Lauren was finishing her breakfast and slipping cornflakes to Bella and Lucy, who were sitting on either side of her chair.

"Morning, Mrs. Woods," he said politely to Lauren's mom. "Um, I was just wondering if Lauren wanted to come out and play."

"I'm sure she does!" Lauren's mom said, looking delighted, and Lauren rolled her eyes at Sam, who tried not to laugh.

"I guess I'm popular," he said quietly as they went across the yard with Lucy and Bella on their leashes.

"Mom thinks it's really nice for

me to have a friend living close by." Lauren swallowed nervously. "Sorry I haven't been very friendly. I was a little annoyed when Mom arranged all the carpooling—I didn't have a choice."

"Me too!" Sam agreed. "My mom kept going on about how lucky I was, and I was like, she's a girl and I've never even met her! Sorry," he added. "Anyway, I've got a plan!"

"You do?" Lauren asked eagerly. "Tell me."

Sam sat down on the rusty old tractor that had been abandoned on the edge of the field, and beamed. "I think we should buy Lucy ourselves! I've got fifty dollars of birthday money left. I'd give you that, no problem, if I could sort of share Lucy. Take her for walks sometimes and stuff. It's the closest I'll get to having a dog, after all."

Lauren nodded slowly. "I've got the money my grandma gave me at the beginning of summer, since I've been so busy with the puppies that I never got around to spending it. That's seventy-five dollars so far. Puppies can't cost more than a hundred fifty dollars, can they? But how are we going to find the rest of the money?"

Sam grinned. "I thought we could pick the apples from the orchard and sell them. We could set up a stall on that big patch of grass where the lane down to the farm ends. It's close enough to the road for people to see us and stop."

Lauren jumped off the tractor wheel.

"That's a great idea! Mom and Dad never have time to pick them, so they won't mind. I'll go and get some buckets."

It took a while to pick the apples, since a lot of them had wasps in them, and had to be thrown on the compost heap, but eventually they had three buckets of really nice-looking ones. Lauren grabbed a handful of freezer bags from the kitchen when they went back home for lunch. Sam found an old folding table in the big shed at the back of the cottage, and he borrowed one of the boxes from the move to make into cardboard signs.

Then Lauren had another idea. "You start selling the apples. I just remembered that Mom's always saying I should clear out my old stuffed animals. We can sell those, too. Here, you take Lucy. I'm going to sneak back home and get them."

By the time she struggled down the lane with a trash bag full of plush bears and dogs, Sam was looking very pleased with himself. "I've sold three bags! That's three dollars!" He'd made signs as well, and tied a couple onto the bushes on both sides of the road.

apples
$1

"Awesome! Help me put out the toys on the grass at the front of the table. They're bound to make people look."

"Lucy and Bella have been making people stop, too—they've gotten lots of attention."

It turned out the toys were almost more popular than the apples. Lauren even had to go back and find some more stuffed animals that she hadn't been planning to get rid of, but she didn't mind giving up her Beanie toy dogs if it meant she could keep her real one.

"How much have we made?" Sam asked as they packed up at dinnertime.

"Thirty-five dollars!" Lauren beamed. "So that's one hundred ten altogether. And there's tons more apples we can pick. But I don't think I have any more old toys."

Lauren's mom and dad were so pleased she was getting along with Sam that they didn't ask what they'd been doing all afternoon. And they didn't mind at all when she and Sam and the dogs disappeared again the next morning.

It was the middle of the morning, and they were doing quite well, when a car pulled up by the stall.

"Would you like some apples?" Sam asked, sounding very professional, and the man smiled and dug around in his pockets for some change.

"Actually, I'm looking for Redhills Farm," he explained as Lauren handed the apples through the car window.

"It's down there." Lauren pointed down the lane.

"Thanks. I'm here to look at a beagle puppy—is that the mom? She's beautiful." He nodded at Bella, who was sitting by Lauren's side. He couldn't see Lucy, since she was curled up asleep, half inside Sam's sweatshirt.

"Y-yes . . ." Lauren stammered, and the man waved and drove away.

Sam and Lauren stared at each other in horror. The man had come to buy Lucy! They were too late!

Chapter Eight

"What are we going to do?" Lauren whispered. "We can't let him have her—we can't! Mom didn't say anyone was coming. He must have just showed up."

Sam nodded. "We almost have enough money, too. It's just not fair."

Lauren looked at him, frowning. "If Lucy's not there, he can't see if he likes her . . ." she suggested slowly.

"You mean we should just stay here?" Sam asked.

Lauren shook her head. "No. Because he saw us, and Mom knows we have Lucy. We have to hide. Come on!"

"Where are we going?" Sam asked.

"I don't know yet. Let's just get away from here."

"Okay." Sam zipped up his hoodie and used it like a bag to carry Lucy while Lauren grabbed Bella's leash.

Lucy woke up as they ran back down the lane, since Sam was jiggling her around inside his sweatshirt. She gave an indignant squeak, and tried to wriggle out.

Lauren turned back. "I'll take her— she'll be quieter with me. Shhh, Lucy!" Lucy snuggled gratefully into Lauren's arms as Sam handed her over.

As they peered around the corner of the barn, they saw the man's car parked in the yard. The top half of the back door was open and they could see him talking to Lauren's mom in the kitchen.

"Let's hide in the barn," Lauren said quickly. "If we go behind the bales of straw, we'll still be able to see if they come out."

They sneaked through the open doors and settled themselves at the back of the barn.

"Shhh! I can hear my mom," Lauren whispered.

"Lauren! Lauren!" They could just see Lauren's mom, looking a little embarrassed. "She's probably in the orchard, playing with Lucy," she said.

"I'm sorry, I should've called first," the man said. "I saw the ad and thought I'd just drop in, since I was coming this way. There were two children up at the top of the lane with a beagle."

"Oh! Well, that would be Lauren and Sam. I hope they haven't gone along the road—Lauren knows not to. I'd better go up there and find them. You stay here and finish your drink."

Lauren sank back behind the straw bales. "She's going to be upset when she finds we aren't there," she said slowly.

"Do you want to let your mom know where we are?" Sam asked.

Lauren chewed her lip uncertainly, but then Lucy woke up again inside Sam's hoodie and wriggled out. She gave a little yap and looked up at Lauren with her big brown eyes. She looked so adorable that Lauren knew she couldn't bear to let her go. "No," she said firmly. "He'll give up waiting soon, hopefully."

Lucy climbed off Lauren's lap and went sniffing around the floor and nudging up against Bella, who was sensibly curled up on a pile of straw. Bella yawned and licked Lucy half-heartedly. It looked like she just wanted to sleep.

Lucy could smell delicious smells all

around the barn. She pattered off around the edge of the bale to investigate, and Lauren and Sam both dived to grab her, which made Bella bark.

"Ssshhh!" Lauren hissed, putting her finger to her lips, and Bella gave her a confused look. "Sorry, Bella, sweetie. But we have to be quiet, okay?"

Sam put Lucy in his lap and started to wave a piece of straw for her to chase. "I don't think we can keep this little one quiet, though," he said as Lucy squeaked delightedly and growled at the straw.

"They might not hear from out there. Oh, there's Mom. She looks a little worried," Lauren said guiltily.

Lauren's mom went into the house, and obviously told the man she couldn't find Lauren and Lucy, because he came out and got into his car.

"I'm so sorry," Lauren's mom said.

Lauren thought the man looked disappointed, but she was more worried about the anxious look on her mom's face.

The man handed Lauren's mom a scrap of paper. "Here's my phone number, anyway. Give me a call about it." Then he drove off down the lane.

Lucy growled at the straw again. Sam had stopped waving it around, and she was getting bored. She whined loudly, and tugged the hem of Lauren's jeans with her teeth. She wanted them to play with her.

"Should we come out, now that he's gone?" Sam asked.

Lauren wanted to, especially since she could hear her mom calling for her dad, who was working in the office at the back of the house. Now they'd both be searching for her. But she shook her head. "What if they just call the man to come back?" She nibbled her nails. "I think we have to give it a little longer."

They could hear Lauren's mom and dad going around the house shouting her name. Finally, Bella started whining. "I know, Bella," Lauren whispered. "I'm hungry, too."

"I'm starving," Sam muttered, and then he gasped as he heard a different voice. "That's my mom!"

Sam's mom came running into the yard carrying Molly. Molly was crying and calling, "Sam?"

Sam and Lauren exchanged a guilty glance.

"I'm sorry, I'll have to go out. Molly looks really upset. . . ." Sam was getting to his feet. "You stay—I'll say I wasn't with you."

"It's okay, I'm coming, too," Lauren told him. "And I promise you won't get into trouble. I'll say it was all my idea." They crept over to the barn door and peered out anxiously. Bella looked around their legs, unsure about what was going on. Only Lucy was happy, and squeaked excitedly to see everyone.

"Sam!"

"Lauren!"

"Didn't you hear us calling you? We've been shouting and shouting!" Lauren's mom hugged her. "We had no idea where you were!"

Molly struggled down from her mom's arms and ran to hug Sam.

"Were you in the barn the whole time?" Dad asked, looking from Lauren to Sam and back again.

"Um, yes . . ." Lauren admitted.

"So you were hiding on purpose," Dad said.

Lauren glanced worriedly at Sam, and then said, very fast, "That man had come to buy Lucy, and I didn't want him to."

Mom blinked. "He was very nice. He already has one beagle, and wanted another. He was really disappointed when we couldn't find you."

"Sam, I can't believe you frightened us all like that," his mom said, upset.

"I think we'd all better go inside," Dad said firmly. "I want to understand what's going on here." He shooed Sam and Lauren and the two dogs into the kitchen, where Bella and Lucy went eagerly to their food bowls. "Sit down, you two. Okay. Explain. What was wrong with that man that made you decide to do something so silly? He seemed like he'd be a really good owner."

"Nothing . . ." Lauren began haltingly.

"It wasn't him," Sam put in. "We didn't want anyone to have Lucy. Look." He dug in his hoodie pocket and brought out the old pencil case he'd been keeping the money in.

"One hundred thirty-three dollars," Lauren said proudly as he emptied it onto the table.

Dad frowned. "I don't get it."

"We were going to buy Lucy ourselves!" Lauren explained. "I really, really don't want to sell her to some stranger! We thought a puppy probably costs about a hundred fifty dollars, and we were so close to having that, and then the man came! We had to hide Lucy away in case he got her first!"

"Does this have something to do with the table full of apples set up by the road?" Mom asked.

Lauren nodded. "We sold the apples from the orchard, and my old toys, too."

"And it's my birthday money."

"And my money from Grandma."

"There's more apples left," Sam added. "We should get to a hundred fifty, easily."

Mom smiled sadly. "That man was going to pay six hundred fifty dollars. That's what a pedigree puppy costs."

"Six hundred fifty!" Lauren whispered in horror. "We'll never make that much. Oh, no . . ." And she started to cry. She was going to have to give Lucy up after all.

Lucy looked up from her bowl. What was the matter with Lauren? She dashed across the kitchen floor and scrabbled frantically at Lauren's legs.

Lauren reached down and picked Lucy up, cuddling her close, while Sam petted the puppy's head.

Lucy howled loudly, joining in with Lauren's sobbing.

"Lauren, shhh . . ." her dad said gently. "And please tell Lucy to hush, too—I can't hear myself think. That's better," he added as Lauren petted Lucy and shushed her. "We didn't realize you were that desperate to keep Lucy. Why didn't you say so?"

"I tried!" Lauren burst out. "But you kept saying we had Bella, and ever since the puppies came you'd said we couldn't keep them. I told Sam about it, didn't I?"

Sam nodded. "But we thought if we

had enough money we could keep her. Lauren said I could share her, too."

"Oh, Sam . . ." his mom said sadly. "He loves dogs," she explained to Lauren's parents. "But his dad is allergic."

Lauren's mom was watching Lucy snuggling up in Lauren's arms, her eyes switching from person to person, as she tried to follow what was going on. "She is a nice dog," Mom said slowly.

Lauren's dad looked over at her. "You're the one who didn't want another dog, Annie!"

"Somehow I can't imagine being back to just one, after all those puppies. It already seems so quiet, with only Bella and Lucy." Mom smiled. "And she's definitely the prettiest of the litter."

"So can we keep her?" Lauren asked,

not quite sure whether that was what her mom was saying. "Really? You mean it?"

Mom nodded, and laughed as Lauren hugged her, squishing Lucy in between them. "Don't crush her!"

"But if Bella has puppies again, we're not keeping any!" Dad said sternly.

Lauren shook her head. "Oh, no—I promise I wouldn't even ask!"

"You can have your birthday money back, Sam," Lauren's mom said, smiling.

Sam nodded, but he looked a little sad.

"Do you still want to share Lucy, though?" Lauren asked, holding Lucy out to him.

Sam nodded eagerly, and Lucy

wagged her tail so fast it almost blurred, and then licked his hand lovingly.

"We can use the apple money to buy her a really nice new collar and leash instead of using Bella's old one," Lauren suggested. "And we can put 'This dog belongs to Lauren and Sam' on her collar tag."

Everyone laughed, and Lucy howled again, a real show-off howl with her ears thrown back and her tail wagging under Sam's arm.

Sam grinned. "I think she likes that idea."

SO MANY PERFECT PUPPIES - COLLECT THEM ALL!